ORIGINS OF A GUILD MASTER

ORIGINS OF A GUILD MASTER
A THAUMORIAN LEGENDS NOVELLA

THAUMORIAN LEGENDS
BOOK ZERO

A. M. ENO

DEAR READERS AND REVIEWERS
A NOTE FROM THE AUTHOR

Recently, especially in the Indie Author community, there has been a lot of discourse surrounding negative reviews and how authors have responded to them.

This is a quick note to let you know that my books are, and always will be, a safe space to leave honest reviews - positive or negative. As the author, I promise never to respond to, share, or vilify any reviewer for leaving negative thoughts regarding my work.

That being said, thank you to everyone who has given my work a chance, and I hope you enjoy the adventure you are about to embark on!

Sincerely,

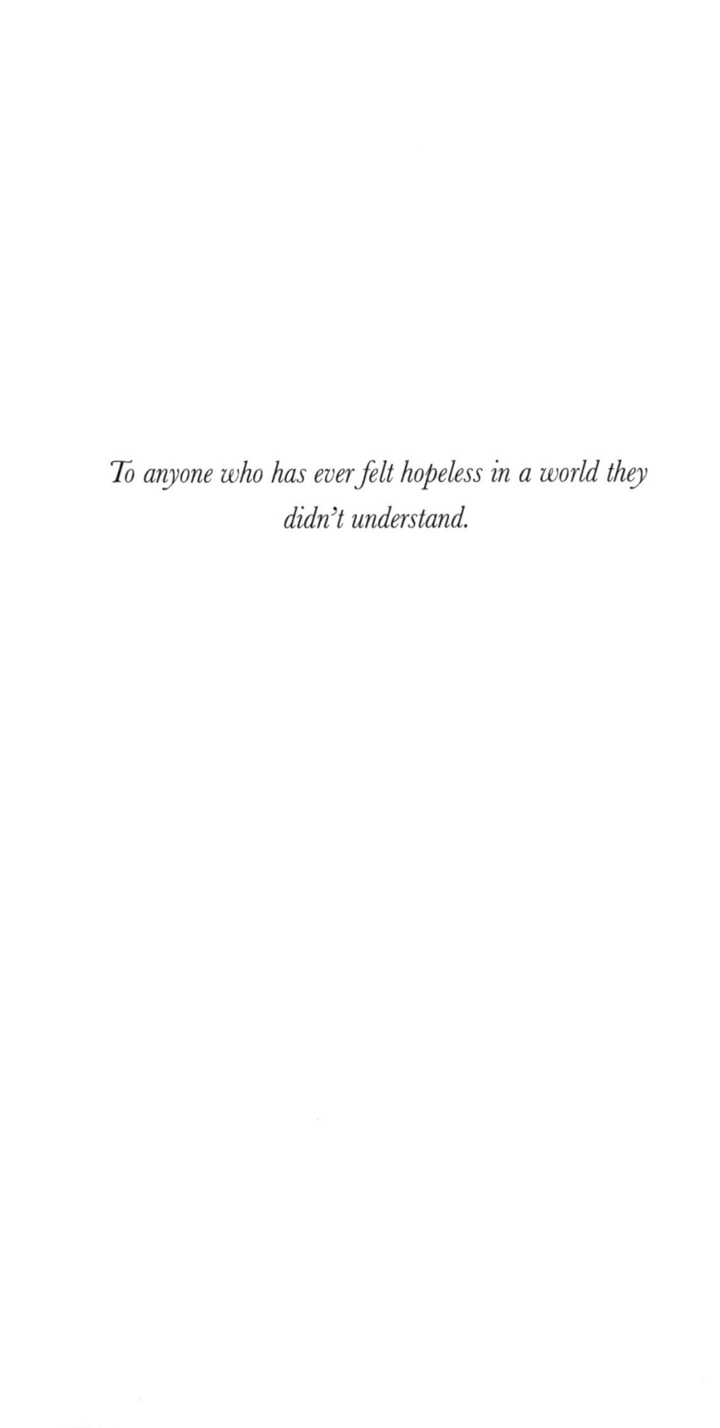

To anyone who has ever felt hopeless in a world they didn't understand.

CHAPTER I

In every speck of magic flowing through Malachi's veins and fueling his continued existence, he felt how furiously slow the clock on his father's desk ticked. Each minute movement of the hands, every cog grinding against one another, occurred ever so slowly. It grated on his nerves as if the mechanisms scraped at his brain. The temptation to reach out with his magic and turn those gears faster grew each second. Perhaps it may even speed up time itself.

Unfortunately, that was not how time worked, so instead, Malachi drummed his fingers against the arm of his chair in time with the passing seconds. The open hardback book in his lap went unread, the horrible clock ticking away, monopolizing his attention.

Tick, tick, tick…

It would be so easy. He would not have to lift a finger. He could reach out with his magic and throw the thing at the wall, shattering it into a hundred unmoving, *silent* pieces.

Of all the Kinetic inventions, clocks were by far the worst. For people with less sensitive magic, they were perfectly bearable. But for Malachi, the continuous, non-stop, minuscule movements plucked his every nerve.

Tick, tick, tick…

At the exact moment the hands hit the hour mark and the device chimed, the door behind him opened, making him jump and his magic brushing against the timepiece lurch. The clock flew across the desk and broke into a dozen mechanical pieces as it smashed against the wall.

A familiar sigh came from behind him, and Malachi shifted in his chair guiltily.

"I apologize," Malachi mumbled. Snapping his book shut, he sat up straighter.

Approaching the desk, Malachi's father

took care to step over the broken clock pieces and deliberately settle in his chair, his mother following in after and perching on the arm. Unconsciously, his father's fingers brushed across his mother's back, grazing up and down her spine.

"Thank you for meeting with us today. We have something to discuss with you," his mother started, her voice somewhere between motherly and formal. Her business-like tone was something she rarely wielded, making beads of sweat form around the collar of Malachi's shirt.

"As you know, we were supposed to meet with several business owners in the City of Elementals."

Malachi's father appraised him, leaning back without ever taking his hand off his wife. Despite the formality of the discussion and the Kinetic society as a whole, they seemed unable to keep from showing affection.

"However, something came up in the Beck's sector of the mines, and they have requested my assistance."

Malachi nodded, eager to hear what

would come next, expecting they had also requested his presence.

Exploring the mines, the backbone of the City of Kinetics' economy, was his favorite pastime. The way the darkness enveloped him, the narrow halls hugging him close. There was an inherent danger to the mines and being so far underground, but it did not lessen the sense of safety and security he got when enclosed in blackness. For Malachi, being underground brought about the same feeling as that of a child hiding under blankets or locking themselves in a closet during a fit. Something about the small space sheltered him from the pressures of the outside world.

"I see. Would you like me to contact the City of Elementals and let them know there has been a change of plans?"

The offer came out rushed, excitement propelling Malachi's words. The urge to get underground made him antsy.

"Actually, dear," his mother shifted. "We decided you should go in our stead."

Malachi blinked once… twice. A deafening silence blanketed the office, roaring in his ears. Clearing his throat, he uncrossed and recrossed his legs until he entirely repositioned himself in his chair.

"I-I am not so sure…" Malachi stuttered, trying to find the words.

The social part of running the business was never his forte. He was atrocious at it, in fact. Enclosed spaces, paperwork, and brief conversations were more his specialty.

Malachi's mother's eyes softened at his unease. "Your father and I understand this will be outside your regular duties. However, we agree that meeting with prospective partners and buyers is an important skill to develop. You must run the business independently one day, and these duties will be yours."

"Not only that," his father interjected, "but it will be important for you to see how the other cities operate. Each culture is unique, and you cannot sell to those you do not understand."

"I have read every book on the cultural differences between the magic classes and the governmental structures of each city. I understand plenty," Malachi pleaded.

Drinks with business owners, small talk with a governor's son and daughters, and casual lunches with the Lady of the city defined Malachi's worst nightmares. What was wrong with staying in the mines and reading contracts?

A soft smile amplified the pity in his father's eyes. "Son, you cannot understand people through books."

Malachi disagreed, but he realized he was not being given a choice. Despite being an adult, he was also an employee, which meant when his parents gave him a task, they expected it to be done without question.

Sucking on his teeth, Malachi lowered his head in defeat. "Yes, sir. Yes, ma'am."

"Excellent," his mother smiled. "Now go prepare. You will leave first thing in the morning."

Malachi opened his mouth to protest, then shut it again. That would get him nowhere. Standing on shaky legs, book in hand, he started for the door.

His father cleared his throat. "Son." His father raised an eyebrow. "The clock."

Oh… right.

Malachi waved a hand, focusing on each piece that previously worked in unison to form the clock. Putting the device back together took far more concentration than smashing it against the wall, but he had broken it and put it back together so many times it took little effort overall. Each piece fit like a puzzle; metal gears scraped against one another until everything was back in place.

When correctly reassembled, the clock ticked once again, instantly making his jaw clench.

"One day, you will break things so bad they will not be fixable," his mother warned.

Malachi suppressed a scowl. The horrid contraption would never be unfixable. Even so, he smiled at his mother. Noting the gray-green eyes they shared and how his father doted on her without a second thought, he wondered how he could have turned out so differently. He had inherited none of their charm. None of their warmth.

BACK AT HIS APARTMENT, Malachi navigated around stacks of books and paperwork, orga-nized in a somewhat chaotic pattern that only made sense to him. The towering tomes were the only decoration in his otherwise bland apartment for the last five years.

Acquiring unnecessary clutter was not a common habit among most Kinetics. While every person collected something different, their collections were very focused.

Malachi was, as it just so happened, focused on paperwork and books. He enjoyed the structure of them. He could break down every story and contract and analyze them. Malachi could break a page down into sections or paragraphs, and paragraphs down into sentences comprising words he could scrutinize individually.

He liked to organize his life the same way he managed everything else, with systems and routines. Everything in his life fit into a labeled box, able to be filed and categorized.

That was why, when he returned to his room and packed, he simply stared at the empty suitcase he had bought on his way home. The new responsibility did not fit into Malachi's mental filing cabinets. Just starting the packing process seemed like a momentous undertaking.

What did one take when visiting a new place and integrating into an unfamiliar culture? Should he pack to fit in with them or to conform to his Kinetic norms for some level of familiarity and identity?

How did the new adventure fit into his heavily structured life of documents and solitude?

It could not, he decided.

Instead, if it became a regular part of his place in the business, he would have to create a whole new box in his mind. Another slot in his filing cabinet. Something to hold general conversation starters and phrases to practice and pull out at any time to make him seem personable.

Pacing around his apartment, Malachi pointed and waved at various items he thought he might need on the trip, sending them to lie neatly in the suitcase.

His packing only took him half an hour or so, most of which he used to debate which books he would need. He owned few things and even less clothing, so it took most of his closet to fill his new suitcase.

Malachi dreaded the train ride from the

beautiful northern mountainous City of Kinetics to the seaside port City of the Elementals in the east the following day.

On his last sweep of the apartment, he picked up a book about the history of rail systems in Thaumoria and the mechanisms created by an extensive team of Kinetics, Fire Wielders, and Water Wielders, then another on the history and beliefs of the Elementals. For the rest of the night, he studied until finally falling asleep, lulled into unconsciousness by a particularly dull chapter discussing the pros and cons of using a rail system versus seaports to transport agricultural goods grown by Elementals.

CHAPTER 2

Malachi sipped the drink in his hand, though he did not care for alcohol. It made him feel unbalanced and impaired his reasoning ability, but he wanted to be polite to his host. That, and he would need it if he were going to endure any more of this night.

After four nights of such dreadful events, milling around crowded rooms, brushing elbows with the city's elite, and entertaining conversations completely devoid of substance, he gained a newfound respect for his parents and what they tolerated for their business.

"Absolutely not!" His host waved an

excited hand through the air, accentuating the point he was arguing with an animated Earth Wielder. "You cannot convince me that the Serpents would benefit from trading Ari for Oshay! He hasn't made a single target break all season."

The Earth Wielder huffed, rolling her eyes. "You can't be serious. You Fire Wielders always think target breaks are all that matter. Oshay's had way more saves than any other player this season, which the Serpents seriously need. Ari can barely block a boulder."

The night's host, Modac, was an enthusiastic young Fire Wielder who had recently taken over his father's businesses across the Elemental lands. Their business teamed Fire Wielders and Shifters to create the most amazing blown glass creations. Malachi expected Modac to be a man of art and distinction.

Instead, Malachi had spent the last three hours listening to the ludicrous debate.

Malachi winced as he took another sip of his horribly strong drink. The inane sports teams the Elementals obsessed over were the only thing people seemed to talk about at dinners.

To prepare for his visit, Malachi had brushed up on Elemental religion, historically significant lords and ladies, and the state of the economic status given the Lady's latest tax adjustments. All in preparation to discuss why the business owners and government officials should invest in, and partner with, his family's business of exporting precious metals used in specialized mechanisms.

Instead, Elementals only wanted to discuss which teams scored points, "broke the most targets" (whatever that meant), and which players should rise from junior to professional leagues. Malachi could not comprehend the enthusiasm over competent citizens wasting their talents on nothing but a game.

Kinetics took part in games and sporting events. Of course, they did. They were the best way for children to hone their magic. But when the time came, they invested those skills into something useful, like building, creating, or mining.

Modac clapped Malachi on the shoulder,

leaning in close to sputter slurred words in Malachi's face.

"My man, please side with me on this one. We need an outsider's perspective."

Malachi tried not to flinch from the Fire Wielder's acrid breath. Removing Modac's hand from his shoulder as politely as he could, Malachi subtly stepped away from the conversation. "Unfortunately, I believe it is time for me to return to my room for the night. I have breakfast with Mr. Sten from the western farmlands in the morning and must get to sleep."

It was only half a lie. He did have a meeting with Mr. Sten the next day; however, it was not until mid-morning, and he had plenty of time to sleep in. It was simply the best plausible excuse to leave without insulting anyone.

"Of course!" Modac gushed. "I'm so sorry for keeping you." All the words flowed into each other, alcohol muddling the syllables.

The Earth Wielder smiled, nodding politely in Malachi's direction. "It was so nice to meet you."

"You as well." Malachi nodded in return,

but she had already returned to the original conversation, forgetting his presence altogether.

Night settled over the city on his walk home, and a salty breeze wafted off the sea to the east as Malachi weaved down the streets of the City of Elementals. Supposedly, many people found it an intriguing scent. Used to the crisp, cold mountain air flowing throughout the City of Kinetics streets, or the stagnant dirt-infused smell of the mines, though, the sea air suffocated him. The salt stuck to his sinuses, giving each breath the sensation of swallowing brine.

When Malachi finally returned to his room, he took his first deep breath of the night. He had insisted the windows in his room stay sealed, helping block out some of the sea breeze and making it feel a little more enclosed, despite being on the third floor.

Gazing at his likeness reflected by the solid black windows, Malachi pretended he was back underground, this trip finally over.

Shrugging off his jacket, he went to the desk he insisted he needed in his room. Malachi flipped open a book that he had bought on his first day in the city, discussing the history of the sport the Elementals were so focused on. Upon his arrival, it immediately became clear how important the sport was to the people there, and he thought some educational reading would help enlighten him as to why.

It had not.

He was still unable to hold a conversation on the subject. Malachi had yet to make it through the history section to learn the modern-day rules, intricacies, and politics.

Unbuttoning the cuffs of his crisp white shirt, preparing to change into something more comfortable for bed, Malachi read over the back of his desk chair.

Behind him, something clicked and slid, catching his attention.

A young boy straddled his windowsill, halfway into his room, staring wide-eyed at him.

Neither of them moved for an extraordinary amount of time. Malachi probably should have called for someone or demanded the boy climb back out his window, but he could not stop staring.

He was by far the dirtiest child Malachi had ever seen.

Hair matted and the color indiscernible beneath the filth. It might have been anywhere from a dark blonde to a deep black. Various shades of dirt, dust, and salt caked the boy's hollow cheeks. Ratty clothes hung off his skeletal frame, making him look unfathomably young.

The more Malachi thought about the situation, the more stunned he was. He had made sure the window was locked. His room was on the third floor. How was a child hanging halfway through his window? *Why* was a child hanging halfway through his window?

The boy looked equally shocked to find Malachi, despite it being his room.

"What… What are you doing?" Malachi stuttered, unsure how to react.

The boy's mouth opened and closed, then a blush, almost invisible through the filth, climbed his cheeks. "I'm robbing you."

Malachi had no words.

Was that normal in the City of Elementals? Surely not. If it were, someone would have prepared him, whether that be his parents or books, or… someone.

Malachi did not need to shuffle through his mental filing cabinet for something to say, he already knew he had no reference. No one had ever robbed him before. Was he expected to just let it happen? Was he supposed to refuse or fight? He was not much for fighting.

Malachi ran through every option he could imagine, but each ended with the boy empty-handed or possibly arrested.

Instead, he studied the boy, how his bones were visible beneath his taught skin. Suddenly, the urge to ask when the last time the boy ate overcame him.

That simple question sent his mind down a spiral. Had the boy eaten that day? Did he eat something every day? Where was the boy sleeping? Where in the world were his parents? How could they condone their child climbing three stories to steal from a stranger?

Malachi could have asked all the questions he wanted but would not learn a thing unless the boy trusted him.

Malachi pulled a handful of coins from his pocket, comprising a couple of Kinetic silvers and various Elemental coppers. He held out his hand, an offering of peace and trust.

Skeptical, the boy stared.

"This is all I have on me," Malachi offered.

Malachi was unsure what he expected to happen next, but the coins lifted out of his hand and floated mid-air. Before then, he had not considered the boy being Kinetic a possibility. That a Kinetic child lived like that anywhere in Thaumoria was such a foreign concept he could do nothing but watch the coins clumsily hover across the room and into the boy's outstretched hand.

The world tilted beneath Malachi's feet.

In the City of Kinetics, people had voted a council of representatives into power to think through problems logically and efficiently. They thought as a collective, making decisions that benefited the whole. The people and the city worked together the way gears turned each other in an engine. They moved around each other seamlessly, knowing precisely who they were, their purpose in the community, and where they were going. No person was without training, schooling, or services.

The Kinetics had even debated going coin-free within the boundaries of their city, but ultimately kept them for trade with the rest of Thaumoria. But money was almost inconsequential there. Sure, it traded hands, but few people cared about prices. The collective ensured they never went without if someone did not possess enough to pay for what they needed.

Starving children were not a thing in the City of Kinetics. Unskilled people were unheard of. The idea that some children had such a poor grasp on essential magic? The possibility never entered Malachi's mind.

Before Malachi said another word, the boy slipped back out the window.

It took a full moment for Malachi to realize what was happening. When he did, he raced to the window, horrified at the prospect of the boy falling to his death.

Head hanging out into the night, Malachi watched the boy climb down the side of the building, head swiveling, on the lookout for passersby. When he reached the ground safely, he darted into the dark, never looking back.

CHAPTER 3

For the rest of the night, Malachi thought of nothing else. The encounter repeated incessantly in his mind. He debated everything he could have said or done differently. At some point, Malachi wondered if he imagined the entire thing. The salty breeze blowing through the window he never closed assured him it had all been real. He stared at that window all night, waiting for the boy to return, though he never did.

What else was there for Malachi to do?

At one point, Malachi debated running out into the night and finding the boy, offering him everything he had brought with him. But Malachi knew he could spend the entire night searching the city without covering even a fraction. He did not know the first thing about where a child like that would go or live.

By the time the sun rose, Malachi had convinced himself the boy had been on death's door, so thin his bones were poking through his skin. That if Malachi had not handed over the coins in his pocket, the boy might have starved to death right there in his window.

Was it ludicrous? Absolutely. But the combination of shock and sleep deprivation made his mind reel.

At some point, Malachi nodded off, waking just in time to dress and make it to his mid-morning breakfast meeting.

Between gulps of coffee, he did his best to say all the right things. "Yes, Mr. Sten, of course, we test all materials before sending them off to customers," and, "No, Mr. Sten, I did not attend the games last night; please elaborate."

The entire meeting passed in a haze as Malachi disregarded yet another drawling conversation about the importance of practice schedules when Mr. Sten muttered something that caught his attention.

"It's quite disappointing that the Suns have moved their training ring this year. Of course, in theory, putting such a lucrative spectacle in that part of town should bring money to the area. But what respectable person wishes to walk through such a dangerous area to watch the practice?"

Mr. Sten cut through a piece of meat on his plate, hardly considering his words as he rambled on, but what he said made Malachi's ears perk up.

"Sure, any proper gambler attends at least one to get an idea of how the team looks. But it isn't worth the safety of my coin purse."

Choking on his third cup of coffee, Malachi cleared his throat and eyed Mr. Sten carefully. "I apologize, but did you say part of the City of Elementals is known for thieving?"

Mr. Sten shrugged, glancing up from his plate.

"Of course, boy. The city degenerates must go somewhere. It only makes sense they congregate away from proper businesses and contributing citizens."

He had responded as if it were common sense, but Malachi could not imagine what that would look like. No such place existed in the City of Kinetics. It would not be ethical or efficient.

Undoubtedly, the Elemental people could see how failing to use all their people to their fullest potential was a blunder on the Lady of Elemental's part, and all the lords and ladies who came before her.

"I see," Malachi responded, using his napkin to wipe at the corners of his mouth, feigning indifference. "And how would one get to this part of the city?"

That made Mr. Sten pause and look up from his food, and Malachi realized he had committed a social faux pas.

"What business do you have there? Aren't the goods your family sells quite… pricey?"

Malachi wiped his mouth to hide biting his lip, trying to devise a reasonable excuse.

He nodded, clearing his throat. "Yes. But as a visitor to the city, I like to ensure I avoid anywhere that might be… dangerous," he stumbled over the excuse, sounding inauthentic even to his own ears.

Before the previous night, he would have questioned how an area could be dangerous simply because its citizens were less wealthy, but now he had an idea.

That placated Mr. Sten, however, and he immediately returned his attention to his plate.

"Obviously. I'm surprised someone hasn't warned you yet." Mr. Sten then listed several areas and street names in the order of what he perceived to be the likelihood of losing one's coins.

Shortly after, Malachi excused himself, ending the meeting early under the premise of needing to prepare for a lunch meeting when, in reality, he had no other obligations until dinner. Mr. Sten seemed unfazed, appearing equally eager to end the meeting with someone who could not debate whether the Hawks should replace their long-time, aging director with a younger one.

Malachi repeatedly recited Mr. Sten's directions in his head, listing them off on his fingers until he turned down the first street.

The directions weren't extensive, but he had to walk a long way before recognizing the street names. Apparently, all his meetings were in a part of the city as far from the "degenerate" area as possible.

Just thinking the word made him cringe.

Slowly, the surrounding city changed. At first, the differences were subtle. Buildings needing paint or windows with cracks. But the further he walked, the more the state of the streets made him uneasy. What started as buildings in mild disrepair turned into complete neglect of the people themselves.

Malachi struggled not to stare at the first person he passed sleeping on the sidewalk, their back pressed against a crumbling building, but it did not take long for that to become a regular sight. The salty air turned sour with human odor, and he had to watch his step to avoid stepping in trash piles.

Soon, it was Malachi who became the odd one. Eyes watched him as he walked through the streets, noting his gray three-piece suit and freshly polished shoes. He constantly adjusted his sleeves to keep from glancing over his shoulder. There seemed to be more people outside the dilapidated buildings than in them, and it took all his focus not to stop and stare at the wasted potential around him.

Malachi was about to turn around, intending to find the first street that would take him anywhere else when he spotted a familiar small figure. Hunched where a stoop met brick was the boy who had climbed through his window the night before.

The boy looked even more malnourished in the light of day. He wore the same clothing, practically falling apart at the seams, and so stained it was impossible to tell the fabric's original color. The boy had no shoes, his feet even dirtier than the rest of him (if that was even possible), and his toes laid at odd angles as though they had been attached wrong.

The boy spotted Malachi simultaneously, fear overtaking every feature on his hollow face.

The boy did not wait to see Malachi's reaction. The instant they recognized each other, he sprinted down the street.

For the first time in Malachi's memory, he did not think before he acted. He chased after the boy, not caring about the stares they drew, especially since no one stepped in to stop the pursuit. He followed the boy down one alley and then another, never quite catching up. They ran until Malachi gasped for breath and the streets changed again.

There, the buildings were bigger, the streets emptier. A less residential and more industrial area, though equally run down.

The boy turned another corner, and Malachi followed just in time to see him slip through a rusted door. The door slammed, a lock grating into place as Malachi reached the handle. He yanked on the door anyway, simply out of frustration, and tried to catch his breath.

Internally, Malachi berated himself for not thinking his actions through. Scaring the boy had not been his intention. In fact, he had wanted to offer help.

But a door kept them mere feet apart, and the boy had locked him out. Out of what, exactly? A building that looked like it would fall apart at any moment? Unbelievable.

Malachi's first instinct was to walk away and leave the boy alone. That would be the polite thing to do.

Actually… the polite thing to do would have been not to chase the boy in the first place, but that opportunity was long gone.

Malachi needed to walk away if he wanted to maintain any semblance of the manners drilled into him by the Kinetic City and his parents. He should return to his room and prepare for dinner. Then, an image of the starving boy flashed through his mind, and he could not bring himself to leave.

The city had failed him and had clearly failed so many others. If Malachi helped even one person and proved they had worth if invested in, he could confidently sit down and engage in rational conversation with the Lady about introducing a new way of addressing poverty.

Malachi walked up and down the wall, inspecting various broken windows and calculating the feasibility of climbing through them. There was not even one he imagined himself fitting through without tearing himself or his suit to shreds on the jagged glass. The door would be his only way in.

He grabbed the handle again and pulled, hoping it would miraculously be unlocked.

It was not.

Malachi closed his eyes and pressed his forehead to the cool metal. Steadying breaths helped calm his racing heart, and instinctively, he reached for his magic. It was a calming presence within him. Always there and ready to be of use.

He let it flow unbridled, breathing in time with him as though it were a living being. Pushing the magic out, he extended it into the door, letting it first slide along the exterior before delving deeper into the metal itself. Similar to how Kinetics found precious metals in the walls of the mine, Malachi used the explorative nature of his magic to analyze not only what the door was made of but its inner workings.

It was a ritual so familiar it helped ease his mind.

Instinctively, his magic searched for something movable to latch on to, finding nothing until it reached the hollowed-out section where the locking mechanism rested. The familiar shape of gears beneath the stroke of his magic instantly comforted Malachi as he, by nature, wanted to push and pull the hardware.

Malachi jerked at a sudden idea. That went against everything he believed to be proper. But if it was the only way…

He closed his eyes again, concentrating.

His magic once again worked along the inner mechanism of the door's lock, learning how the gears fit together and the shape of each piece. Running through his mental catalog of every basic lock he knew, Malachi tried to match one to the one he sensed within the door. He had never contemplated picking a lock before, but it could not be more difficult than reassembling a clock.

Malachi decided on the closest mechanism, understanding what needed to move in what way to unlatch the door, and started meticulously rotating pieces. He rarely used his magic on something he could not see, but it was possible. It took far more concentration and understanding of locking mechanisms than he imagined it would, though.

Eventually, the lock disengaged, and the door yielded. Malachi slipped into the dark building beyond, closing the door behind him.

CHAPTER 4

It took a moment for his eyes to adjust to the shadowy interior, but the odor hit him immediately. It was the stench of tightly packed, unwashed bodies. So over-whelming, he nearly walked right back out to shield himself from it.

Dozens of hushed voices created the white noise surrounding him. No conversation was discernible, though he was confident he was the focus of more than a handful of them.

Through the shadows, he realized the building was one large, open room. People of all ages and magic classes filled the floor from one end to the other. More eyes than he cared for focused on him, and a few stood, closing around him.

The understanding that he was somewhere he was not supposed to be suddenly overtook him. He had been uncomfortable on the streets, drawing more attention than he liked, but in the building, he felt outnumbered. It was the first time he truly understood what Mr. Sten had been talking about when he called the part of the city dangerous.

The closest thing to kindness coming from those near him was closer to concern. Concern for his coin purse. For his safety.

For his life.

"You don't belong here, boy," a deep voice growled from one of the bodies nearby.

Malachi could not agree more with that voice.

"I… there was… I am looking for…"

Malachi tripped over his words. His mind raced, jumping from one threat to another. Tried to keep calm and failed.

A lyrical voice cut through the wall of people around him. "That's enough."

Immediately, everyone reacted, stepping back and giving Malachi space. They parted, making way for a woman to pass. Despite wearing the same ratty clothes as those around her, she was utterly striking. Her presence palpably occupied space, forcing others to step aside.

She took deliberate strides forward, her golden-flecked eyes not bothering to glance at those around her, all her attention focused on Malachi.

Utterly paralyzed beneath her glittering gaze, terror kept him from moving should she vanish into the illusion she must be.

She reached out and ran the back of her fingers down his cheek, an intimate action that should have seemed intrusive but was instead comforting. A lover's caress entirely out of place with everything else going on.

"Who are you looking for, dear?" she cooed, her sweet voice low and alluring.

Malachi's mouth went dry, struggling to remember why he had entered the massive building.

"Uh… I was following… a boy."

The woman laughed, sweet and sensual. "Well, we have plenty of those, love. Any particular one?" She waved a hand as if displaying the surrounding people. As if they were hers to offer.

Malachi glimpsed the boy between bodies, staring wide-eyed and terrified.

Malachi nodded in his direction. "Him."

He was unsure why, but Malachi felt his words condemned the boy, like he should have said nothing. He should have claimed to have entered the wrong building and walked away without a word.

Someone grabbed the boy by the collar, hauling him into the ring of people. The boy stumbled, barely catching himself before regaining his balance. He stared at Malachi's shoes, trembling.

The woman stroked the boy's dirty hair, gazing at him affectionately as though he were a pet. Coyly, she glanced at Malachi from the corner of her golden eyes.

"He is a cute one, isn't he?" she purred.

Malachi did not know how to answer. Sure, children were cute, if sticky and annoying. But he would not classify the young man before him as such, especially not with how underfed he appeared.

Nodding hesitantly, Malachi felt he was agreeing to something he did not understand.

The woman gave an approving hum, studying the boy again.

"How much?" she asked.

The seemingly random question was so abrupt Malachi was unsure they spoke the same language.

"Excuse me?"

The woman looked at him, eyes hardening, the gleam darkening. She annunciated her words as if he were too dense to understand the question. "How. Much?"

Malachi looked around for help from the others, for some clues to what the woman was talking about, but found no helpful faces.

"For what, exactly?"

The woman shrugged, seeming to contemplate the answer. "An hour."

An hour... what in all of Thaumoria could that mean?

The boy flinched, his trembling growing so bad Malachi was sure he would shake himself to death.

She took his silence with offense, eyes

narrowing. "Will that not be enough? Will you need more?"

Malachi wanted to scream that he did not know what she was talking about. Clearly, she was expecting him to pay for something. To offer a deal. He got the sense that offering an acceptable amount was the only thing that would get him out of this situation. He thought about what was in his coin purse and what he could go without.

"A silver. A Kinetic silver." He tried to say it confidently but knew he had done something wrong when the woman's eyes went hungry, whispers rising around him.

"A *silver.*" She said the word as if tasting it for the first time. "What'll you be doing with our boy here that would warrant a *silver?*"

Do with him? Malachi did not plan to do anything with the boy. He just wanted to leave.

The question seemed to be from a place of pure curiosity. It was clear the negotiation was over. She wanted Malachi's money and would give anything for it.

"He… stole from me."

The woman tipped her head back and

barked a laugh that rang around the building. It sent a shiver beneath Malachi's skin. There was no warmth to that laugh, all coyness gone. It was a borderline evil chortle, delighting in pain and wanting punishment.

The boy's breath quickened, knees buckling.

"I see," she sneered, not at Malachi but at the boy. She grabbed a fist full of his hair, and he cried out in pain. "You see what happens when you get caught, you little shit? Now, you do as you're told to make up for it." The woman tossed the boy at Malachi's feet, and when she looked at the boy again, her eyes lost all the affection they previously held.

She stretched out her hand, clearly waiting for the payment Malachi had so stupidly offered. When he placed the single silver coin in her hand, she snatched it away so fast he was tempted to count his fingers to ensure she had not taken one of those as well.

"You have an hour," she told him. "Don't call the guards, and I won't check for blood when you bring him back. Deal?"

Malachi opened his mouth, letting it hang open, unsure how to respond.

The boy whimpered at his feet.

Malachi swallowed hard. Did they think he was going to beat the boy? He had never struck another human being in his life. He could not even recall striking a pesky insect. Malachi would never, no matter what, hit a child.

But that was not what they wanted to hear. Not what they expected from him. So Malachi nodded. "Deal."

The boy's shoulders caved in, his entire body folding.

"Good. Typically, gentlemen use the alley, though for a silver…" the woman mused.

Malachi shook his head. Somewhere out of sight, away from prying eyes, was what he needed. "The alley is fine."

"Excellent." The woman placed a foot on the boy's back and shoved him forward. "Show him."

The boy cried but nodded, falling against the door and entering the light. Malachi followed closely behind, desperate to be out of the building and away from the woman staring at him like something to eat.

He shadowed the boy, who trudged silently

away from the door. The boy trembled, never looking higher than the dirt directly before him. They had not gone far when the boy turned a corner, leading Malachi down a narrow, dark alley filled with discarded crates, boxes, and other trash.

When they reached the enclosed end, the boy turned and waited.

Malachi stood awkwardly out of arm's reach, unsure what to do. He did not know what he had agreed to or bought.

Had he indeed paid a silver coin to beat the boy? He hoped not, but no alternative came to mind.

"I am sorry," Malachi said; at the same time, the boy blurted, "I've never done this before."

Malachi stilled, brow furrowing. "Never done what before?"

The boy shifted from foot to foot. "Pleasured," he whispered. "But I've heard stories from the other boys who have."

Suddenly, the contents of Malachi's earlier meal threatened to find itself on the alley ground. The boy could not possibly mean…

"You… you paid for an hour," the boy

stuttered, still not looking up, clearing his throat before adding, "With no checks." Tears rolled down his cheeks. He seemed to force the words out. He pulled at the hem of his ratty shirt, lifting it with shaking fingers.

"No!" Malachi screeched louder than he meant.

The boy jumped as though being struck. Or expected to be.

"No, no, no, no…" Malachi could not stop repeating the word, as though the repetition made everything better. As if the boy would not understand it the first time or even the fifth. "No. No, no. Please do not remove anything. No."

Finally, the boy looked up, hopeful but confused. "But you paid for—"

"I did not know." Malachi interrupted, the words spilling out faster than he could catch them. "I did not mean it. I would never touch you like that. I would never touch you at all. It was a mistake. Please, I am so sorry."

Malachi felt he should get on his knees and beg for the boy's forgiveness. Then, it occurred to him that he had been the only one lost during that negotiation. That woman had *sold* the boy to Malachi for… "pleasure." She understood what was happening and looked eager to hand over the child for a coin.

Malachi was not a rageful person, but his vision went red. He could have marched right back to that room and torn every person to pieces. It was such a foreign feeling Malachi stumbled back a step, as if the urge had physically assaulted him.

The only thing stopping him was the horrified boy before him. So many conflicting emotions crossed the boy's face. His thought process of trying to understand what Malachi was saying was evident across his features.

"Then… you would like to use a belt? For a beating?"

Malachi's eyes almost popped out of his head. "Never! Please understand I do not wish you any harm. I only wanted to help."

The boy's brows furrowed, scrunching so hard it looked almost painful. "You paid the Mistress… to help me?"

Malachi sighed, holding his head in his hands. "I paid because that was clearly what she wanted. I did not understand what I was paying for. If I had, I never would have agreed. Never."

"Oh," the boy whispered.

The two of them stood there in silence for a long while, unsure where to go next in the conversation.

Malachi only had one question. The same question he had been asking himself since he first laid eyes on the boy.

"When was the last time you ate?"

The boy's face twisted in confusion, as though he did not understand the significance. He shrugged. "I don't know."

"You do not… how do you not know?"

The boy shrugged again.

"What about the coins I gave you? Did you not use them?"

The boy shook his head. "I didn't have enough."

"Not enough?"

Malachi was indignant. That was impossible. The boy could have eaten well for weeks on what Malachi gave him. At least once a day for an entire month, had the boy been smart about it.

"How is that possible? Where did it

go?" Had the boy wasted Malachi's generosity?

"I had to pay the Mistress," the boy said, like it was the most obvious thing in the world, as though it were Malachi saying odd things.

At that moment, Malachi realized how little he understood about the world. He could have read every book in Thaumoria without being prepared for that moment. The skinny, dirty, malnourished boy stared at him the way one would stare at a creature who did not comprehend the need to breathe.

The boy understood more about the inner workings of the city than Malachi ever could.

"Why would you pay the Mistress?"

"She takes care of us. That's how guilds work."

Guild. A word Malachi knew, but not within that context. As defined by his dictionary at home, a guild was an association or society. He had always affiliated it with a particular company or group of workers.

From his observation, that building did not work like an association or company.

Or had it?

Had Malachi not negotiated with the

person who ran the company? Had he not paid for goods and services despite not knowing what those goods and services were? Was it not common for those who ran the company to take a commission on what others earned?

Malachi was trying to understand and keep up with all the new information he was learning. "Help me understand. You steal things and then give them to your Mistress as a commission?"

The boy shrugged. "I guess."

"Then what does she provide you?"

"She takes care of us," the boy repeated, not seeming to see the disconnect.

"How? You do not eat. You do not bathe. She sold you for a silver coin to be abused. How does she care for you?"

The boy nodded along to Malachi's list as though it were normal, to be expected.

"She allows me to sleep there. No one in the guild can hurt me or take my things. I keep what she doesn't take," he said it all so matter-of-factly, almost condescendingly.

Malachi paced. "How much of what I gave you were you allowed to keep?"

The boy rummaged through his pockets and pulled out four copper coins, holding them out for Malachi to see.

"That is all? I gave you silver as well."

Malachi wanted to yell. To scream at the top of his lungs for all to hear the horrid injustice.

The boy nodded. "She took those. They were the first silvers I ever brought back, though. So, I got my own bed in a corner for that."

The boy smiled with pride as though this were the most incredible thing he could imagine achieving: a bed in a corner that he was not required to share.

Malachi's heart shattered. Fell apart with such a painful tear he was surprised he did not collapse right there in the alley. Tears filled his eyes at the boy's pure joy at the thought of his new bed. That was all it took to make him happy—a new bed on the floor in a slightly better spot. How hard was his life for something so small to be considered a reward?

The Kinetic boy who could barely use his magic, who could not remember the last time he ate, who should have been living a life full of education and relative luxury.

The boy noticed Malachi's tear-filled eyes, and concern returned to his face. "What? Do you think I should've gotten something better? Like… a mattress?"

Malachi swallowed back his tears, refusing to let them fall.

"I think you deserve so much more."

The boy broke out into a gap-toothed grin. "Maybe I can rob you again and get a loaf of bread."

Malachi ignored the pain shooting through his chest and smiled back. "I could buy you one."

The boy's eyes went so wide they filled half his face. "Really?"

"Of course. Where is the closest bakery? Is it far?"

The boy shook his head, excited. "Not at all. Just a few streets over. They've got the good stuff, too. Stuff that isn't hard."

Malachi's breath hitched in his throat as he struggled to hold back the flood of emotions threatening to consume him.

Instead, he pressed his quaking lips together to maintain a smile.

"Let us go then."

The boy skipped out of the alley, genuinely excited. Malachi's long legs easily caught up, and they walked side by side down the street, away from the Mistress's building.

Malachi watched the boy, thinking it was nice to see him smile. He wondered how long it had been since the boy had last smiled.

"What is your name?" Malachi asked.

"Eu. What's yours?"

"Malachi."

Eu stopped and stuck out his hand. "Nice to meet you, Malachi."

Malachi took Eu's hand and gave it a gentle shake. "Nice to meet you, too, Eu."

CHAPTER 5

Eu practically inhaled the sandwich Malachi had purchased for him. He had had it topped with everything the skeletal boy requested, resulting in an absolute mess that Eu licked off his fingers (after Malachi insisted he wash his hands, of course).

Their hour was almost up, and the two returned to the Mistress's building, talking the entire way.

Eu was curious, asking questions about the City of Kinetics, Malachi's life, and everything in between. The various inventions from the City of Kinetics and the development process particularly intrigued him.

It was clear to Malachi that, despite having little connection to the Kinetic way of life, the boy examined the world the way a Kinetic would. With pinpoint curiosity, striving to understand the way things worked and how to fix problems with a strategically logical approach, the boy asked questions about the internal mechanisms of train engines, curious how magic and science worked hand-in-hand.

By the time the Mistress's building came into view, they had moved on to the daily operations of the mines.

"So, your family runs the mines?"

Malachi shook his head. "No. Technically, the mines belong to the city and the council that runs it. My family purchases a share of one of the mines and what comes out of that section. We then sell that back to the city to supplement further innovation or to business owners and inventors in other cities. That profit pays our researchers, who tell us the most profitable sections of the mines, and various other employees who extract the material, refine it, and more."

"Wow…" the boy whispered, lost in thought. "And what do you do?"

"I read over contracts, business statements, and other forms of paperwork to ensure all the technical aspects are taken care of."

He did not mention that he would have preferred working in the mine as part of the research team. After all, that was how his family had started in the mining business. They were so successful at what they did, coming from a long line of powerful and sensitive Kinetics, they eventually funded an entire branch of the mining operations.

However, businesses worked better when their wealth was distributed equally, meaning they had an obligation to employ as many people as possible, returning their profits to the community. That meant the family stayed in their place, behind desks, making sure others had their fair share of work and opportunity.

As much as Malachi understood that, and all the other economic theories, it never stopped him from dreaming of the mines. Of walking into the dark and letting his magic mix with his instincts, feeling deep into the rock in search of the precious metals they desired.

Eu's face screwed to the side. "Well, that sounds boring. You should get a better job."

An unbidden laugh bubbled out of Malachi. "Maybe."

The two stopped when the door to the building came into view. Dread filled Malachi's belly, making him sick, but Eu seemed indifferent. That was home to him; he had walked down the narrow street hundreds of times and had nothing to fear.

He had a new bed waiting for him.

Only Malachi understood there was more out there. That his living situation was inadequate and should never be considered normal.

"I guess this is it. See ya, Malachi." Eu waved, resigned to his lot in life.

"Eu," Malachi called, halting the boy. "I will be in the city for the rest of the week. If you would like, you may… rob me again."

Eu gave him a toothy, genuine grin that stretched from ear to ear. "Really?"

Malachi nodded once. He could not bring

himself to speak, fearing his voice would quiver.

"Okay! Thanks." Eu ran to the door, knocking before slipping through.

Malachi did not stick around. He turned and walked away, not wanting another meeting with the Mistress. Should they meet again, things would get ugly. Malachi was not a fighter, but if there was ever a person he wanted to harm, the woman who sold him a child for a coin was at the top of his list.

FOR THE FOLLOWING FIVE NIGHTS, Eu appeared in Malachi's window at the same time without fail. Each night, Malachi prepared an array of food for Eu. He ensured there were various choices, from nutritious meals to treats from the best bakeries he could find. Eu would pick a handful of things, leaving Malachi with the rest, and the two would sit and talk for hours.

Eu's curiosity never ceased. He came prepared each night with questions for

Malachi about everything and anything he could think of.

One night, they talked about nothing but stories and books. Eu could not read, but had heard about various titles and wanted to know every detail. When he ran out of stories to ask about, he started asking Malachi to describe every book he had ever read, from fairy tales to anthologies.

The next night, Eu wanted to know about the different cities, eager to understand how they ran and learn every detail about the people. Why did the Anima abstain from eating meat if that was what they exported? How did Witches get accepted into the University, and why did their council only select apprentices from the school's program? Did the High Sage of the City of Shifters truly not claim a gender identity? How did that work?

Malachi was exhausted by the time Eu left each night. Feeling as though the boy had squeezed every piece of knowledge Malachi had from his brain, leaving him drained but pleasantly curious himself. Frequently, they would reach a point where Eu would ask more than Malachi knew, and Malachi had to promise to research the topic and present what he learned the next night.

On the fifth night, after Eu filled himself on that night's selection of dishes, it was Malachi's turn to ask a question.

"Eu, would you ever consider leaving the City of Elementals?"

Eu shrugged without looking up from the array of treats sitting out. "Not really. I don't have a choice."

"Why is that?"

"I don't have any money."

Malachi sighed. Eu left with a pocket full of coins each night, and the next night, they were gone.

Over the week, Malachi came to understand exactly how the Mistress ran her guild. People presented what they made each night, and the Mistress would decide how much the people owed her for the right to continue sleeping in her building. Malachi had yet to figure out what gave the Mistress the right to decide who may or may not live in her building, but it was clear no one questioned it.

Living in the building was safer and more

comfortable than living on the streets, and if you were a favorite of hers, she would also provide you with work. That had intrigued Malachi until he learned the work was always much like what he had paid for when he had unwittingly handed over a silver coin. "Pleasuring," Eu had called it, though, from his description of how people returned from their work, it did not sound all that pleasurable for those being sold. The more money changing hands, the more willing the Mistress was to look the other way regarding her employee's safety.

"But if you had the funds, would you leave?" Malachi pushed.

Eu thought about it more, tilting his head from side to side. "Maybe. Some of those places sound pretty cool."

"What about the City of Kinetics? Does that sound… pretty cool?"

The boy nodded, mouth full of a flakey pastry.

Malachi wrung his hands, knee bouncing. "How would you feel about returning to the City of Kinetics with me when I return home?"

When Eu left to return to the Mistress's care each night, Malachi feared he would never see the boy again. What if someone decided the boy's life was less important than the coins Malachi gifted him? And what would happen when Malachi left and Eu no longer provided the Mistress with the coins she expected?

There were so many unknowns, and Malachi could not help but look at the boy before him the way a Kinetic approached any problem. He thought of each part of the problem individually. He considered how they worked together and how he could fix each piece. Eventually, Malachi came to one conclusion. Unless the boy returned with him to the City of Kinetics, Malachi could do nothing to continue helping.

Eu froze, eyes going wide. "Really? Like… to live with you and go to school and work in the mines?"

"I… possibly." All the answers to those questions were so different. "I cannot promise we would live together or that you would work in the mines. But we would care for you, and you could control your future. You may become an inventor or get elected to the council."

"I could do that?" Eu's voice was quiet and unsure, as though he had considered none of that possible.

Malachi leaned forward, nodding, wanting to reach out to assure Eu it was, in fact, true. The offer was genuine. In a few days, Eu's life could be forever changed. No more wondering where his next meal would come from. No more handing over everything he made just to ensure a corner to sleep in. No more fear of being sold to a low-life creep who would take advantage of his situation.

But Malachi did not want to push too far and scare Eu away or make him feel pressured into doing something he did not want to do. So he kept his hands clasped before him, willing them not to shake.

"Yes. With the right opportunities, you could do anything you set your mind to. You are a bright boy who deserves a chance to show Thaumoria what you can do, Eu. If you come to the City of Kinetics, your future will be bright."

Eu was quiet for a long time. Malachi

could practically see the thoughts running through his mind, wheels turning.

"But I wouldn't live with you?" The boy's voice wavered, fear and uncertainty coating each word. His life might not be comfortable or safe, but it was familiar, and what Malachi offered had to be terrifying—filled with the unknown. Knowing he would live with Malachi would give him something solid to hold on to, something familiar.

But Malachi was not prepared to care for a child. He knew nothing about raising someone or helping them become their best selves. He lived in a small apartment with room for one. Malachi had never come close to marrying, meaning Eu would not have a mother. If he entered the council's custody, they would find him a place in a loving home. People who wanted children and had been preparing for this for years and would care for him.

But Eu did not know that. That was just another unknown.

Could Malachi take him in? He could afford a bigger apartment, could he not? It would thrill his parents to have a child to spoil, but what about the day-to-day? What did Malachi know about caring for children? Nothing. He knew nothing. They needed food, water, safety, comfort, and care. Security. But there was more to it than that. There had to be.

"I do not think I would be the best caregiver…"

Eu's shoulders slumped, and Malachi swore the boy's future was slipping through his fingers with each word.

"However…" Malachi started, and Eu perked up. "We could entertain the idea of me caring for you until we find a more permanent home."

Eu nodded slowly, taking everything in. "Yeah, okay."

Malachi clasped his hands, anxiously rubbing his palms together as he shifted in his seat. "Okay?"

Eu nodded again, more sure of himself. "Yes. I'd like that."

All the tension Malachi did not know he had been experiencing melted out of him, relief relaxing every muscle in his body until he slumped in his chair, smiling like a giddy child.

"Wonderful. That is simply wonderful." Malachi's approval made the boy smile more, his toothy grin beaming. "This is excellent, truly. We will leave the morning after tomorrow. I have to visit with Lady Aladonna tomorrow night."

Eu sat up a little straighter, his excitement growing with each passing moment. Practically bouncing in his chair, he jumped up and hugged Malachi, wrapping his arms around Malachi's neck.

Stunned, Malachi froze, unsure how to react. He was not used to much physical contact, even from his parents, but he could not stop the sudden warmth spreading through his chest as the boy clung to him.

Malachi reached up and patted Eu on the back, letting himself relax into the hug, pulling the thin boy closer as he did, not caring about the dirty clothes.

Malachi could not think of a moment prouder than that one.

He was going to do it. He was going to save Eu's life. It gave him all the confidence he would need to face the Lady tomorrow. To reveal the reality of what was happening in her city to her and convince her of the improvements that needed to happen.

For several nights, Malachi had been thinking about how if he could save Eu, he could do anything. He could help so many others.

Malachi pulled away, holding Eu by the shoulders, unwilling to let him go just yet. He blinked away the tears pooling in his eyes, his happiness and relief overflowing, needing a release.

"You can stay here until we leave. I will have a room made up for you next door."

Malachi had already thought of that as well. Earlier, he had questioned the inn owner and convinced them to keep the neighboring room empty in case Eu agreed and needed a place to stay until they left.

Eu pulled back, shaking his head. Tears of joy streaked his dirty cheeks. He wiped them away with his palms, leaving his face splotchy with dust and red spots. "But I have to get my stuff. I need to say goodbye."

"Oh…" Malachi had not realized the boy owned anything, though it made sense his belongings would be precious to him if he did. "Then gather your things, and the room will be ready when you arrive. Though this time, how about you use the front door instead of the window?"

"Ok," Eu agreed, tears continuing to fall despite the smile on his face. "I'll be back soon. Promise." He hugged Malachi again, quicker than the last one, before darting to Malachi's open window.

Malachi laughed as the boy climbed back out the window, despite how unnecessary it was. Apparently, some habits would be hard to break. But that was fine by Malachi.

Malachi went to the lobby and paid for the room next to his, requesting things be made up immediately with the inn's best linens and pillows. He oversaw everything, ensuring things were exactly how he wanted them for Eu's arrival.

Long after the maid finished, Malachi stayed in the room, waiting. Every so often, he would stand and rearrange something. Shift the chair a few inches to the left. Straighten the pillows yet again. Ensure that no dust had settled on the end table. Re-count the towels to ensure none went missing since the last time he counted.

Hours passed until, eventually, Malachi fell asleep in the room's cushioned chair. When he awoke, the sun was high in the sky. The morning came, and the perfectly made-up bed remained empty.

Eu had not returned.

CHAPTER 6

Alarms went off in Malachi's head, and he continued to sit in that chair, counting off the seconds in his head. When the sun rose to mid-sky, he accepted that something was keeping Eu from returning.

Malachi washed and dressed quickly. He checked in with the front desk, ensuring Eu had not returned and been turned away, but they claimed not to have seen the boy.

Before he knew it, Malachi was venturing through the streets of the City of Elementals, head on a swivel, eager to glimpse the familiar head of matted hair. He did not think it through as he headed towards the Mistress's building, no longer bothered by the cramped streets, trash-filled gutters, and loitered corners.

He no longer experienced the city as Mr. Sten described it. Instead, Malachi saw people funneled into an area to be hidden from the rest of Thaumoria because no one wanted to deal with them. Indignation on their behalf fueled his determination to find Eu, return to his rooms, and prepare to give Lady Aladonna the tongue-lashing she deserved for failing her people. Her status as the Lady of the Elementals did not give her the right to treat them so poorly; it was her duty to give her best to them, and Malachi intended to tell her as much.

When he found himself once more before the rusted door to the Mistress's building, he considered forcing the lock again, but decided civility would be a better approach. So, he knocked three sharp strikes that stung his knuckles.

A large man with a scraggly beard opened

the door, staring down at Malachi with beady eyes.

"What?" the man asked, gruff and uninterested.

"I am looking for someone. I have reason to believe I will find them here." Malachi tapped his foot, impatient. He was not in the mood to play games or answer to anyone.

The man's eyes narrowed, looking Malachi up and down. "Who?"

Malachi resisted the urge to roll his eyes. "Does it matter? I need to find them immediately."

The man grunted and slammed the door in Malachi's face. Malachi blanched, pounding on the door with the side of his fist when the shock wore off. When no one answered, his impatience won out, and once again, Malachi used his magic to manipulate the lock on the door.

He slammed it open, prepared to face the large man again, but found himself looking down into a familiar, striking face.

"Well, well, well... the gentleman returns," she purred.

Malachi would not fall for the seductive

part she played again. He glared at her. "Where is Eu?"

She tilted her head to the side, lips lifting in a mockingly innocent smirk. "I haven't seen our friend since last night."

"You lie."

The Mistress stepped back, waving a hand at the building, granting Malachi entrance. "Have a look for yourself."

Malachi slowly made his way deeper into the building, stepping between bodies curled up on the floor, buried under blankets filled with holes and covered in stains. Despite the salty, thick air hanging heavily within the building, they all appeared content beneath their coverings, sweat intensifying the stench of so many unwashed bodies. Few stirred as he passed, but those who did, stared, analyzing every inch of his person.

He would have judged them for choosing such poor living conditions a week ago. But he had learned how it was the better option, and that knowledge made his temper flare. These people were being taken advantage of. Their coins stolen, an education withheld, all so they did not have to sleep on the streets, exposed to the onslaught of weather the Elemental City was known for.

Malachi made his way to each corner of the building, remembering what Eu told him about his reward for bringing back silver coins. Various items and people covered nearly every inch of the floor, but one corner appeared conspicuously empty.

Layered blankets created a makeshift mattress, neatly arranged. There was no doubt in Malachi's mind it was Eu's bed.

Despite their smell, part of Malachi wanted to gather the blankets, hold them close, and take them with him. Eu cared for the ratty things, and Malachi could not imagine how hard he had worked to obtain them.

Another part of Malachi wanted to tear them to shreds. It was painfully clear to him no one had slept there recently, which meant Eu had not returned for his things.

He was not there, and Malachi was unsure where else to look. Those neatly stacked blankets represented Malachi's failings, which he wanted to destroy.

There was nothing left to do but return to his rooms at the inn and hope Eu returned.

Kinetics were not religious. They did not believe in gods or goddesses or deities the way the other magic classes did. But in that moment, Malachi understood the need to believe. He desperately wished he could fall to his knees and pray to a being more powerful than himself. Beg them to step in and bestow some level of benevolence upon a child who deserved a better chance at life.

But if they were real, if an all-powerful being existed, then they were yet another being who had failed Eu. Who was to say they would help now?

A sensual voice broke through Malachi's musings. "It's a shame, really. He was quite cute. So much earning potential."

Malachi whirled on her, towering above her petite form. He wanted to intimidate her, wanted her to flinch, but she was unaffected by his looming.

"How dare you?" he growled. It was a sound he had never produced before. It came from somewhere primal, deep within him, fueled by the memory of his last encounter with her.

You don't call the guards, and I won't check for blood when you bring him back.

Her metallic eyes sparkled at his anger. "I'm afraid I don't know what you're referring to."

"You sold him to me. You would not have cared if I beat him half to death or even…" Malachi could not bring himself to say the words. "Even if I had… violated him. You would not have cared."

She shrugged. "Why would I? You paid enough to cover his dues for years to come. If he hadn't returned… well," she shrugged again. It was such a callous, indifferent movement at odds with her beauty.

Malachi wanted to throttle her. To force her to care and understand the implications of what she had done. What she continued to do.

"You *sold* him!" Malachi's vision blurred at the edges, honing in on nothing but the creature before him.

She leaned in close and spat, "And you bought him. What makes you any better?"

"I…" Malachi started, but promptly cut off the words. He what? He did not know?

Malachi knew he was paying for something wrong, but it had not stopped him. Of course, he had not understood the full scope of what was happening, but money still exchanged hands. He still paid the woman. Still took part in the horrific practice.

Malachi looked around, realization striking him.

It was a horrific practice. He could not deny that. Selling another human being against their will was vile. But how many eyes staring back at him were still there because of the trade? How many had no other option and used their bodies, their only thing to sell, to purchase their last meal? Who was he to judge what they did to survive?

Malachi could scream and yell at the top of his lungs all day long. He could grovel and educate and offer all the solutions in the world. But the reality was he was leaving in the morning, and where would that leave these people? Right there, doing the only thing they knew.

Without greater change, nothing he did, no amount of his anger, would help anyone.

Malachi did not respond to the Mistress. She deserved no more of his time.

He stormed out of the building, blindly navigating the streets until he returned to the inn. He checked with the desk, with no genuine belief there would be any positive news, but he needed to know, anyway.

Eu still had not returned.

CHAPTER 7

The carriage ride to the Lady's estate took a lifetime. There was nowhere Malachi wanted to be less that night, but he would not pass up the opportunity to speak his mind to the woman responsible for the last week.

When his carriage pulled up, he was one of many to start his journey up the steps to the massive double doors standing open for the guests to enter. It was not a private dinner; they would never consider Malachi such an important person. Instead, it would be a night filled with copious amounts of food, drink, dancing, and gossip.

Just the thought of such opulence made him ill.

A servant escorted him down the halls of the manor, walls covered in an abundance of installations from the City of Shifters. Around every corner, the manor dripped with color, luxury, and art. They had spared not a single corner.

He considered what he had learned about the City of Elementals before his arrival. Power and strength were the basis for their government system. A magic duel, won in an arena, determined the right to rule. While heirs were often plucked off the streets at a young age, their power easy to identify from birth, and raised alongside the current lord or lady, anyone who thought they could defeat the lord or lady had the right to issue a challenge.

It was so different from how the Kinetics ran their city that, prior to his arrival, Malachi had struggled to imagine how such a system worked. Having witnessed how the least powerful lived, he understood the manor for what it was: a show of strength. It was a way to rub mightiness in the face of those born less fortunate.

Being born with lesser magic was not their fault. In fact, how much of that "lesser magic" was just a lack of training? How many less fortunate were only less fortunate because no one wanted to give them a chance?

Malachi silently seethed as he entered the ballroom, immediately struck by the smell of a wide array of rich foods. Typically, the scents would have made his stomach growl with anticipation. Instead, it simply kindled his anger.

Not too far away was a boy thrilled at the chance to eat bread that was not stale. With overflowing tables lining the walls with an uncountable number of steaming dishes, he could not bring himself to desire any of it.

Malachi scanned the room, eager to find the Lady, speak his mind, and return to the problem at hand. He would not leave the city without Eu.

He found her milling through the crowd, her height making her easy to spot.

Lady Aladonna was a duel-wielder, as the Elementals called it. She could wield both air and water, a rare gift. In a city of thousands, few were dual-wielders and even fewer tri-wielders. She was one of the heirs raised within the manor, always knowing her destiny.

Like most air wielders, she had a lanky form, accentuated by a long, form-fitting dress pooling at her feet. Her other element, water, gave her a languid stride and brilliant blue eyes. She was beautiful and elegant, and Malachi hated her.

He hated what she stood for. Hated her lack of policy. And hated the privilege granted to her from birth.

Malachi strode forward, not bothering to glance at those around him. He should have acknowledged the familiar faces filling the crowd. Business owners he had met with throughout the week. His initial goal was to flatter. But he did not care if he gave them a simple greeting.

In no time, he found himself before Lady Aladonna. She radiated power and grace, and when their gazes met, his confidence wavered. It made him acutely aware of his position in Thaumoria and that he had no business scolding the Elemental Lady.

That would not stop him, though.

The Lady dipped her chin. "Hello there. Have we met before?"

Clearing his throat, he swallowed the urge to shout his irritation. "Not yet, though I hope to change that."

She held out her hand, and Malachi took her fingers in his, bowing slightly to show his appreciation for her status. "Malachi Starik, my Lady. It is my pleasure." The words were acid on his tongue, but he needed her to listen, and a lack of courtesy would not benefit him.

"Mine as well." She looked Malachi up and down, taking in his usual gray suit and pale green eyes. "Are you a transport to my city or simply visiting?"

Malachi forced a smile. "Visiting, my Lady. In fact, I wished to discuss some significant differences I noticed between our beloved cities with you."

She laughed. Actually tipped her head back and chuckled. "Malachi, please. This is a night of relaxation. Business and policy should be the furthest thing from your mind. Enjoy the night and leave word with one of my advisors. We can discuss such things another time."

The Lady turned to engage in another discussion, but Malachi would not let her ignore him so easily. He placed a hand on her arm. A brazen gesture that caught her attention.

Her features stayed smooth and relaxed, but her eyes blazed. Had she been a Fire Wielder, he imagined those eyes would have scorched him.

"Unfortunately, I intend to leave in the morning, and this is quite important. Please grant me a moment of your time."

She glanced down at his hand still on her arm, a clear warning, but he did not remove it. He needed her to listen.

"How about a dance, shall we?" Her voice carried something hard. She was offering the span of a song to speak his mind and nothing more.

Malachi nodded. "Of course."

Music faded, leading into the next song, as he led her onto the dance floor. He had one song to convince her. One song to do what he came to do. He would need every second.

The Lady stepped into his arms, eyes never leaving his. As the music flared to life, they stepped. It was an unfamiliar song, but the Lady was easy to lead, even taking over at points to ensure they did not fumble.

"Speak quickly," she whispered, low enough for only him to hear, but the threat in those two words was loud and clear.

"Are you aware people in your city are suffering while others are swimming in wealth?"

She snorted, looking around the lavish room. "Is that what this is about? Did the businessman from the 'city of opportunity' take a trip downtown for the spectacle?"

Malachi glared at her, not caring who watched. "Spectacle? People are starving. A boy broke into my room for a few coins so he may eat."

A part of him expected that to hit the Lady hard, but she seemed completely unaffected by such a statement. "I apologize for the inconvenience. It is a nuisance my guards have been attempting to address." She said it all with a bland connotation, as though delivering unpleasant news about the weather.

"Are you truly so heartless?" he snapped. Her burning gaze whirled on him, but he could not bring himself to care. "Children are starving on the street. Kinetic children. Elemental children. Do you not care? They are selling themselves, so they may have a roof over their heads."

"What would you like me to do about it, Mr. Starik? Clearly, they have no respect for the opportunities this city presents, and I have no control over the situations they were born into. I was born with power. They were not. I cannot change that."

"And what are these opportunities you speak of? They are undoubtedly ineffective if so many die within sight of a bakery that could have saved their lives."

The Lady shook her head, irritation flaring. "You act as though half the city were starving. I assure you, it's a tiny proportion of my people on the street corner."

Malachi did not miss the fact that she had avoided his question. "Even one child on the street corner is too many."

"Then you are welcome to take them home with you." The statement was so casual he wondered for a moment if she suspected he had already offered, only for said child to go missing.

"I am certainly trying."

That caught her attention, and she watched him closely as she spun under his arm before returning to face him. "Trying? And they are not willing to join you?" That possibility seemed to amuse her. As though it proved a point of some kind.

"No. He was happy to come with me, but has been missing ever since."

She chuckled. "Mr. Starik, how can a homeless child go missing?"

Malachi's jaw clenched, teeth grinding. How could she not care? Anger had words spilling out of him, telling her everything, hoping something would sting her.

"He has been living in an abandoned building under the control of a Mistress who sold him to me for a silver coin. Like you, she had no care for his safety or health, but unlike you, at least she provided him some basic human needs, such as a bed." Calling a corner filled with blankets a bed was a bit of an exaggeration, but he wanted the Lady to understand just how wholly she had failed her people.

The Lady seemed to think it over, taking several moments before replying. He could not guess what was going through her mind, but the slightest bit of hope flamed in his heart.

When her eyes met his again, something changed. "I see. And you know where this… Mistress is housing people? Could give directions?"

Malachi nearly sagged with relief. Something he said had affected her. "Yes."

Lady Aladonna nodded thoughtfully. "Okay, Mr. Starik, I will make you a deal. Tell my guards everything you know of this Mistress, and I will help you locate your missing child."

Malachi let out a long breath, some of the tension in his chest easing. It was not quite the result he had hoped for, but it was a start.

"Thank you."

As the song ended, he spun the Lady one last time. They bowed to each other, as was the custom. But before they parted, the Lady caught his attention once again.

"And Mr. Starik?" He met her eyes. "Never touch me again."

The warning was icy, leaving no room to interpret it as anything but the threat it was.

Malachi nodded and turned away, not wanting to waste another moment.

CHAPTER 8

ick, tick, tick…

Malachi stared at the clock in the room that still sat empty, waiting for Eu. He had removed the one in his own room as soon as he'd entered it the first night, but he did not feel it was his place to remove the one there. And, hours after his confrontation with Lady Aladonna, that clock mocked him.

Tick, tick, tick…

He had given every bit of information he could think of to the captain of the City Guard. The location of the Mistress's building, a description of the Mistress herself, a description of Eu, and anything else he could think of. He did not know what he expected, but he had not expected them sending him back to his rooms and telling him to sit and wait.

He had wanted to help. Wanted to be there when they arrested the Mistress and saved Eu. But if Malachi was good at anything, it was maintaining order and doing as he was told. That was the Kinetic way, after all. Things only ran smoothly if people did their job and stayed in their place. An engine could not run if a single gear did not do its job.

So, he listened and returned to his room.

However, staring at that wretched clock, watching the minutes pass, listening seemed to be a mistake.

Malachi was too antsy. Too eager to move. He needed to do something.

Tick, tick, tick…

Without too much consideration for the repercussions, Malachi stood and made his way out of the room, sending the clock flying against the wall as he left.

He did not bother wandering the streets or

pretending he did not have a destination in mind. Malachi hardly noticed the city around him as he navigated, determined to see what was keeping the guards and Eu for so long.

Malachi was so focused on his destination and lost in his own world, he did not notice the panicked people until he collided with one of them. The man, hurtling down the street and ramming into his shoulder, pulled Malachi from his fantasies.

Looking around, genuinely taking in his surroundings for the first time, people ran opposite the direction he was heading. Distantly, screams and the sound of utter chaos echoed off the surrounding buildings.

He paid no attention to the surrounding swarm. Malachi picked up his pace, hastening toward his destination. The closer he got to the Mistress's building, the louder the chaos, and the more panicked the surrounding people were. The more city guards converged toward one point.

Malachi pushed past the guards, ignoring their shouts of warning. Several tried to grab him, but he gave them no thought. Magic flew from him with little bidding, sending hands, rocks, and other things Malachi did not see flying in the opposite direction. Heart pounding in his chest, he did not care if they did not want him there.

He had to see what was happening.

Malachi froze when he turned the corner that would take him to the familiar rusted door. City guards dragged weeping figures from the building. They pled for forgiveness, begged to be set free, but the guards paid no attention. They lined up each person in the street, one after another.

Malachi scanned each face, but none were Eu.

The only thing keeping him standing was the hope that the Lady would keep her word and would spare Eu.

Only one individual was calm as they were led from the building. A strikingly beautiful human who held her head high, chin jutted into the air as though she were leading the procession.

The Mistress.

Malachi surged forward, not caring who saw or who tried to stop him. He threw himself at the Mistress, throwing her to the ground and landing atop her.

She cried out when she hit the stone, her calm facade finally breaking, and Malachi pinned her shoulders, forcing her golden gaze to look up at him.

"Where is he?" Malachi pleaded, desperation making his voice break.

When the Mistress recognized him, she smiled. A wicked expression that showed no care for herself or anyone else.

"Did you think I'd let such a profit go? That boy was my biggest earner. I couldn't just let him leave," she seethed beneath him.

Hands grabbed Malachi, pulling him off the Mistress and prying them apart. Malachi became a rabid animal, kicking and fighting with all his might.

"What did you do to him?" Malachi screamed. He needed to know. He needed answers.

As the city guards regained control of the Mistress, she whirled, fighting to keep her eyes on Malachi.

"What did *I* do? Look around," the Mistress screeched.

So Malachi did.

He stopped fighting, and for the first time, he honestly observed the eviction.

City guards carried out armloads of items, dumping them on the disgusting ground, creating a pile of dirty rags that had been so precious to those who worked so hard for them. A line of thin, skeletal figures awaited their fate.

That was not what Malachi had wanted. Not what he had intended when he told the captain the address of the building. He had only wanted the Mistress arrested.

He had just wanted to help.

The Mistress was right; it was all Malachi's fault. He had been arrogant, thinking he knew what was best for those people. But he was wrong. Thoroughly and tragically wrong.

He had assumed that if the Lady opened her eyes to what was happening in her city, she would want to do better. Instead, she was exterminating. Ridding her city of the perceived blight, not by assisting but by removing them. Like a witch cutting away a tumor.

Why had he thought she had a sudden

change of heart? Who did he think he was to change anything?

"Mr. Starik," a deep, familiar voice boomed. Malachi found the face of the captain. "I told you, no need to come down. We have it under control." The captain gestured to the guards holding Malachi, and they dropped him.

Malachi nearly fell to his knees without their support, hardly able to hold himself up under the weight of what he had caused.

"Under control?" Malachi balked, fists clenching to keep from visibly shaking. "Do you not see what is happening?"

The captain looked around, proud. "Of course. We try to eliminate these underground operations whenever we get word of them. Businesses like this are terrible for the economy. No way to tax them." He said the words so matter-of-factly that, for a moment, Malachi wondered if that was the way of things everywhere and if he was the one in the dark.

He tried to see the horrifying scene through the captain's eyes. As nothing more than a job. A business. The people as commodities. But he could not. Just trying was revolting.

Maybe… maybe there was still hope. Even just a shred.

In the custody of the city, the people would at least be fed. That, of course, was common practice. They would get… cells. But those cells had beds. Proper beds, off the floor and out of foul weather. Maybe the Lady did not have services in place for the public, but undoubtedly, she provided something to people once incarcerated.

"Do you see your boy anywhere?" The captain's eyes wandered over the amassing crowd, uncaring. He could have been asking after a pair of shoes.

Malachi shook his head, constantly searching.

"You sure? Because I'd hate to get on with things and have it be too late."

Too late… Malachi looked up at the captain, suddenly feeling small. "What do you mean?"

"Well, we have some pretty good witches around here, but no one can bring a lad back from the dead." The captain clapped a hand on Malachi's shoulder and laughed.

Malachi's entire world fell away. The captain could not possibly mean…

"Well, if you're sure?"

Malachi's mouth hung open, unable to find words.

The captain took the silence as confirmation. "That's too bad. Well, no time like the present. Is that everyone?" he asked one of the passing city guards, who exited the building empty-handed.

"Yes, sir. We searched the entire building."

"Good. Let's get this over with."

The guards gathered everyone closer together before backing away to a safe distance. The Mistress stood at the front; her gaze never leaving Malachi's, letting him know what was about to come was his fault.

He had done that.

She never even screamed as the street went up in flames.

EPILOGUE

Malachi walked through the dilapidated building he had just purchased under a fake name. It was falling apart, filled with trash and broken windows. He had considered not purchasing it at all, but something about that felt too wrong. He had to maintain some sense of civility in his life.

The salty air hung heavy around him, but after weeks in the City of Elementals, he grew used to the constant taste of the sea on his tongue.

Returning to the City of Kinetics was impossible after what he had witnessed, what he had caused. The thought of facing his parents and explaining his actions was unthinkable. He wrote them, of course, letting them know he needed to stay longer. He had needed to write that last goodbye, to ease his heart and gain some sense of closer for the life he was leaving behind. But when the weeks passed, and he did not return, his parents would start to worry.

By then, he would have thoroughly covered his tracks, having long since left behind his rooms at the inn and presuming various false names.

His parents would grieve for their missing son. But it was better than them knowing what he planned for the future. That was something two self-respecting Kinetic parents would never forgive.

Turning his back on everything he knew would be one of the hardest things Malachi ever did, but making the decision to do it was easy. No more difficult than destroying a clock.

After witnessing that night's wreckage, Malachi returned to his room and sat perfectly still for an extraordinarily long time. The sight of all those people burning in the street played over and over again in his mind, sending him falling down an internal well of self-loathing.

He thought through everything he had said and done since arriving in the City of Elementals, trying to understand where he had gone so wrong.

Alone in his dark, silent room at the inn, he finally understood his most significant weaknesses: ignorance, arrogance, and avoidance.

Malachi had believed everyone would think the same way he did if he only presented them with information. If he only educated them enough, they would change their ways to match his, as if he knew what was best for everyone. Then, he thought he could sit back and let everyone solve their own problems. All he had to do was open their eyes, and they would take care of the rest.

Every part of that was wrong.

He had been horrifically humbled.

After that night, he understood the world in a way he never thought he would. Understood his place and purpose. If Malachi wanted things to be run differently, he needed to do something about it. Walking away and hoping things worked themselves out was not enough. He needed to be active.

He needed to build something different.

The building would act as the framework for that change. It did not look like much, but that was precisely what he needed. He needed something that would blend in and not draw attention.

Malachi would build his own guild. A place that offered actual services and assistance. He would offer education, training, and everything a person needed to thrive: food, shelter, education, support, and more.

Malachi knew everything about running a business, which was precisely how he would run it.

If the Lady would not listen to him when he said people needed a chance, he would show her. Show her what happened when those she threw away received the chance to become something more.

He would continue looking for Eu, but after two weeks of searching, he had not found so much as a lead to where he may be. Malachi feared the worst, but he had to maintain hope. And if he never found Eu, he would let Eu's memory inspire what he built.

It would be what Eu had never had, what he deserved.

Just the thought of the missing boy made his heart ache. Each night, Malachi sat awake, watching his window until the sun came up and he finally slept. He imagined Eu showing up at any moment, ready to share where he had been. Ready to start his life a new.

Malachi remembered those fateful words his parents had left him with those long weeks ago.

One day, you will break things so bad they will not be fixable.

Truer words had never been spoken, and Malachi had not fully understood what they meant until he watched all those people burn because of him. Malachi could never fix that. He could never make up for such an appalling mistake.

But he would undoubtedly do his best to prove what he knew to be true and build something like no other—and vowed never to make the same mistakes twice.

Acknowledgments

As my first piece of published work, Origins of a Guild Master has taken its toll on me both emotionally and physically. There have been many sleepless nights, emotional break-downs, and the greatest of highs. This novella marks the beginning of what I hope to be a long career as an author, and it never would have happened if it weren't for a team of people supporting me along the way.

First, my ever-patient and understanding husband, Joel, who has stood by my side through some of the hardest times in my life. For holding me while I cried and never letting me forget what I was capable of. He's been my alpha reader, my support team, my backbone, and my cheerleader.

To my family, who never told me to give up and never doubted I could accomplish what I set my mind to. My parents might not get along, but they never wavered in the belief that I was capable of great things. I hope to one day live up to those dreams. Also, my siblings, who don't know it, but have always been a safe place for me in life.

A major thank you to my cover designers at JV Arts, who worked hard to bring my vague descriptions to life and make my books as stunning as could be.

To all my beta readers who built me up when I doubted everything I'd written. And also, my editor, Sydney Rain, who tore my work apart and put it back together again so that it could be the best it could be.

Finally, a big thank you to all my readers. Thank you for giving my work a chance and allowing me this opportunity to impact your world. Without you, this would all be for nothing.

Forever grateful,
A.M. Eno

About the Author

Originally from Howell, Michigan, A.M. Eno travels full-time with her husband and two cats. In 2017, she earned her Bachelor of Science from Black Hills State University, majoring in Psychology and a minor in Sociology. As a lifelong avid reader, she hopes to create worlds and characters that invite readers to fall in love and feel at home. She strives to write high fantasy series that are a safe space for people of all backgrounds.